Library and Archives Canada Cataloguing in Publication

Cole, Kathryn, author
Sign up here : a story about friendship / written by
Kathryn Cole ; illustrated by Qin Leng.

(I'm a great little kid series)
Co-published by: Boost Child & Youth Advocacy Centre.
ISBN 978-1-927583-90-6 (hardback)

1. Friendship—Juvenile fiction. I. Leng, Qin, illustrator
II. Boost Child & Youth Advocacy Centre, sponsoring body III. Title.

PS8605.O4353S54 2016   jC813'.6   C2015-908360-5

*Boost Child & Youth Advocacy Centre gratefully acknowledges the generous support
of Rogers Communications for funding the development and publication of the Prevention
Program Series. Rogers Communications is an important partner in our efforts to prevent
abuse and violence in children's lives.*

*Second Story Press gratefully acknowledges the support of the Ontario Arts Council and the
Canada Council for the Arts for our publishing program. We acknowledge the financial support
of the Government of Canada through the Canada Book Fund.*

Published by
Second Story Press
20 Maud Street, Suite 401
Toronto, Ontario, Canada
M5V 2M5
www.secondstorypress.ca

Sign Up Here

A story about friendship

written by Kathryn Cole
illustrated by Qin Leng

Second Story Press

Fountaindale Public Library District
300 W. Briarcliff Rd.
Bolingbrook, IL 60440

"Hey, Dee-Dee," Lin called, "we're starting a club. It's—"

"Lin!" Claire interrupted. "Dee-Dee can't join. It's a walking club. And…she isn't exactly great at walking."

"No," said Dee-Dee, "but I'm great at trying. Can I just join and do my best?"

"No," said Claire. "Our club is for people who can walk properly. You would slow everyone down. Come on, Lin, let's find somebody else."

Lin looked sorry, but she followed Claire anyway.

Dee-Dee's feelings were hurt. She was sure she could keep up, but Lin and Claire were acting like she wasn't good enough to be with them. Good friends were supposed to be kind, not mean.

Who needs them and their dumb club! I have lots of friends, she told herself.

Some boys were cheering noisily in a circle nearby. Dee-Dee walked over and pushed her way through. There in the middle were Devon and Shaun. They were on the ground arm wrestling. "What's up guys?" she asked.

"You are looking at the first meeting of the Strong-Arm Wrestling Club," Kamal told her.

This sounded like fun. "Where do I sign up?" Dee-Dee asked. She could do this. She had very strong arms from using her crutch to get around.

Everything went quiet. Devon and Shaun stopped wrestling. Then Joseph stepped forward. "If you can beat me," he said, "we'll see about signing up."

Dee-Dee was confident. She got down on the ground opposite Joseph and flexed her muscles. *Easy-peasy*, she thought.

It was! After five seconds Joseph's arm gave out. The boys looked at each other, not knowing what to say.

Finally, Kamal spoke up. "Sorry, Dee-Dee," he said. "But you can't join the *All-Boys* Strong-Arm Wrestling Club…. You're a girl."

Dee-Dee dusted herself off. "You mean I'm a girl, and none of you boys can beat me."

"Dee-Dee wait…" Joseph called as she left, but Kamal stopped him.

"She'll get over it, Joseph. We don't want girls in our club."

Joseph watched Dee-Dee go, and returned to the circle.

"Not good enough for one club and too good for another," Dee-Dee muttered. Now she was hurt *and* disappointed. Kamal had been her friend since junior kindergarten, and he'd never cared that she was a girl. Real friends were supposed to play fair.

Dee-Dee tried to ignore feeling left out, but the next day it happened again! She was crossing the schoolyard when she saw a bunch of kids huddled together. They spotted Dee-Dee, whispered something to each other, and stopped talking.

"What's going on?"
Dee-Dee asked.
 "You wouldn't be
interested," said Nadia.
 "Try me."

"We're starting a pet-sitters club," Shaun told her. "Every week we'll go to a different person's house and learn about their fish or cat or dog or hamster – whatever. Everyone will get to show off their pets and teach the others how to care for them. Pretty soon we'll know enough to be pet-sitters when we're older."

"But I don't have a pet," Dee-Dee said.

"And that's why you wouldn't be interested," Nadia told her.

"I could learn about *your* pets. I could still be a pet-sitter."

"Nope. You have to own a pet to join. That's the rule," said Nadia.

Dee-Dee couldn't believe it. Everybody belonged to something – except her. She felt sad and totally alone. For a second she thought Shaun might say something, but he didn't.

I have to do something to change this, Dee-Dee thought. *Friends shouldn't leave you out. They should try to include you.*

Dee-Dee knew *she* was a good friend. She had helped Kamal to be brave about reptiles.

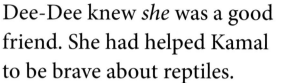

She'd made Lin feel better when her mother's birthday money was lost.

She had shared tips with Shaun so he could keep his balance in gym.

She'd turned Nadia's skipping rope to give everyone a chance at double Dutch. No one cared then about two strong legs, being a boy or a girl, having a pet – or not – before clubs.

She could fix this. She just needed to think. Pretty soon, Dee-Dee had the best idea ever.

She found Ms. Crosby and asked to use some art supplies. "I want to make some signs," she said. "Could you please help me with the words?"

Ms. Crosby was curious. "Probably," she said. "Can you tell me what this is all about?"

Dee-Dee told her about the clubs and how friendships were being spoiled and how upset she felt. And then she told Ms. Crosby about her plan.

"Dee-Dee! How clever," Ms. Crosby said. "Of course, I'll help. Stay with me tomorrow morning at recess, and we will make the signs together."

The following afternoon at recess, Dee-Dee was sitting behind a small table, in front of a big sign that read "Friendship! Sign Up Here!"

One by one the kids gathered around. Lin stepped up first. "How does a friendship club work, Dee-Dee? Who can join?"

"Oh, hi Lin," Dee-Dee said. "Actually, it's not a club, it's just friendship. It's for everyone. You can have one leg or two, be a girl or a boy, young or old, have a bunch of pets or none at all. You just have to treat others the way you would like to be treated, and you can sign up."

"Who'd want to sign up for that?" Lin asked.

"I would," said Ms. Crosby, coming up from behind. "It sounds fantastic. May I be the first?"

"Sure," said Dee-Dee, handing her a pad, a pencil, and one of the smaller signs.

"Be helpful," read Ms. Crosby. "Thanks Dee-Dee. I'll remember that."

"I'm next," said Lin. "I'm sorry I wasn't a very good friend before, Dee-Dee." She chose *Care*.

"Me too," said Joseph, lining up. "We weren't playing fair."

"Me three," added Shaun. "I didn't want to be a pet-sitter anyway. I'm allergic to fur. That's why I have so many fish. You can have some."

Kamal was next. "I should have remembered what good friends we are," he said. "Is it too late to sign up?"

Dee-Dee felt great as her list of friends grew, and the signs disappeared.

She and her friends were back together,
and Ms. Crosby's class was happy again.

For Grown-ups

About Making and Keeping Friends

Healthy friendships are a part of a child's support network. Children with good social supports are less vulnerable to bullying and interpersonal violence. Making and keeping friends is a learned skill, and parents play an important role in teaching children how to make friends. Guiding them to foster good interpersonal skills such as empathy, problem solving, and moral reasoning will help them develop successful social relationships.

Parents can support their children by helping them develop healthy friendships:

- **Talk about feelings:** Discuss emotions in a non-judgmental way – when all children's feelings are validated they are more likely to respect the needs of others.

- **Teach conversation skills:** Practice taking turns and using *active listening* and *I-messages*.

- **Encourage cooperative play:** Kids get along better and exhibit more tolerance when they are engaged in activities that work toward a common goal.

- **Foster empathy:** Demonstrate sympathetic concern for others and discuss how people in different scenarios might be feeling.

- **Talk about conflicts:** Differences of opinion are common to all relationships. Your child may need help working through emotions and solving problems.

- **Build connections:** Provide opportunities to develop friendships in a variety of environments, including school, neighborhood, and extracurricular activities.

- **Model respect:** Respecting others is about treating people the way you want to be treated.